Start Reading Music

by Amy Appleby

A proven, step-by-step method on mastering
the basics of sightreading.

Amsco Publications
New York/London/Sydney

Cover illustration by Sue Grecke
Cover art direction by Kristine Luhrssen
Interior design and layout by Don Giller

This book Copyright © 1992 by Amsco Publications,
A Division of Music Sales Corporation, New York, NY.

Order No. AM 80219
US International Standard Book Number: 0.8256.1246.2
UK International Standard Book Number: 0.7119.2333.7

Exclusive Distributors:
Music Sales Corporation
257 Park Avenue South, New York, NY 10010 USA
Music Sales Limited
8/9 Frith Street, London W1V 5TZ England
Music Sales Pty. Limited
120 Rothschild Street, Rosebery, Sydney, NSW 2018, Australia

Printed in the United States of America by
Vicks Lithograph and Printing Corporation

Table of Contents

Introduction	5
Reading Notes on the Staff	6
The Treble Clef	6
Naming Notes	6
Notes on the Staff	6
Leger Lines	7
The Bass Clef	8
Leger Lines	9
Playing Notes on the Keyboard	11
Playing Notes on Guitar and Other Instruments	12
The Grand Staff	13
The Octave Sign	13
Note Values and Rhythm	14
Reading a Song Melody: Pitch and Rhythm	16
Rests	16
Notes and Rests	17
Pickup Notes	17
Dotted Notes and Rests	18
Time Signatures	20
$\frac{4}{4}$ Time	20
$\frac{3}{4}$ Time	21
$\frac{2}{4}$ Time	21
$\frac{2}{2}$ Time	22
$\frac{3}{2}$ and $\frac{4}{2}$ time	22
$\frac{2}{8}$, $\frac{3}{8}$, and $\frac{4}{8}$ Time	22
Accidentals	23
Sharps	23
Flats	24
Naturals	25
Major Key Signatures and Scales	26
The Key of C Major	26
The Sharp Keys	27
The Flat Keys	30
Compound Time Signatures	32
More about Note Values and Rhythm	34
Ties	34
Extended Rests	35
Pauses	35
Triplets and Other Note Groupings	35
Tempo	37
Expression	38
Dynamics	38
Structure	39
Repeat Sign	39
Inverted Repeat Sign	40
Da Capo	40
Dal Segno	41
Alternate Endings	41
D.C. al Coda	42
D.S. al Coda	42
D.C. al Fine	43
D.S. al Fine	43
Accents and Articulations	44
Staccato	44
Accents	44
Slur	45
Phrase Mark	45
Ornaments	46
Grace Notes	46
Trills	47
Tremolo	47
Turns	48
Mordents	48

Intervals   49
   Diatonic Intervals   49
   Chromatic Intervals   50
Double Sharps and Double Flats   53
Minor Key Signatures and Scales   54
Further Study   60
Answers to Written Exercises   61

Introduction

Whether you are an instrumentalist, singer, or composer, you can take a giant leap forward by learning to read music from the printed page. This book will provide you with everything you need to know to read music—and to communicate effectively with other musicians about standard music notation. By following this proven, step-by-step method, you can quickly master the basics of sightreading—from the fundamentals of melody and rhythm to the subtleties of musical expression and ornamentation.

Learning to read music need not be a dull process of memorizing rules. In fact, you'll find many musical concepts quite easy to understand when you see and hear how they function in familiar songs. Reading music is a practical skill, so its important that you play or sing along as you learn to read. Be sure to obtain a fingering chart for your instrument, so you can play each example in the book. Special exercises are provided along the way to help you sharpen your newfound skills. These also give you a chance to test your ability to read and understand music at each important stage in the learning process.

Reading Notes on the Staff

Written music is a universal language of notes and symbols, arranged on the musical *staff*, which consists of five lines and four spaces.

The Treble Clef

Clefs are symbols that provide a frame of reference for writing notes on the staff. In other words, the clef tells the musician exactly which tones are indicated by the notes occurring on each line and space of the staff.

There are two clefs that commonly appear in written music: the *treble clef* and the *bass clef*. The treble clef is usually used in music intended for middle- and high-range instruments and voices, while the bass clef is used in music written for lower instruments and voices. Let's take a look at the treble clef on the staff.

This clef is also sometimes called the *G clef* because the curlicue of the clef sign circles the second line up from the bottom of the staff. This line marks the position of the G note, and so provides a frame of reference for notes placed on any of the other lines and spaces of the staff.

Naming Notes

Notes are the building blocks of music. Each note usually indicates two qualities: pitch and duration. *Pitch* is simply how high or low a particular tone sounds. *Duration* is how long an individual tone should last. We'll get into note duration in the next chapter. For now, let's focus on how notes indicate pitch.

Musical notes are named using the first seven letters of the alphabet: A, B, C, D, E, F, and G. These letter names indicate notes in an ascending sequence—from low to high. After the final G note, the sequence begins again: A, B, C, D, E, F, G; A, B, C, D, E, F, G; and so on. Most instruments are able to produce a large enough range of notes to repeat this seven-note sequence several times.

The distance between any two notes with the same letter name is called an *octave*. This term, from the Greek word meaning "eight," reminds us that a note's letter name repeats at every eighth tone of the sequence. Although the two tones that form an octave are actually different notes, each tone sounds as if it were just a higher or lower version of the same note.

Notes on the Staff

Here are some notes arranged on the staff in the treble clef. Notice that a note falls on every line and space of the staff. When notes are arranged in a sequence like this they are collectively called a *scale*.

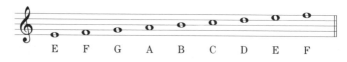

Take the time to memorize the position and name of each of these notes. Then test your ability to identify notes by looking at the familiar folk tune "Yankee Doodle." Write the appropriate letter name in the space provided below each note.

Yankee Doodle

Leger Lines

Now that you are familiar with the notes on the staff in the treble clef, take a look at the notes that extend above and below the staff. The additional lines used to extend notes beyond the staff in this way are referred to as *leger lines*.

Take the time to memorize the position and names of each of these new notes. Then label each of the notes in the familiar tune phrases below. (Don't be confused by the dots and stems, which are covered in the next chapter, "Note Values and Rhythm.")

Aura Lee (Love Me Tender)

Surprise Symphony

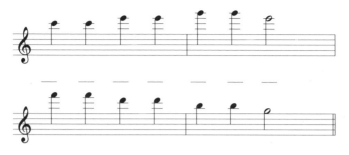

Angels We Have Heard on High

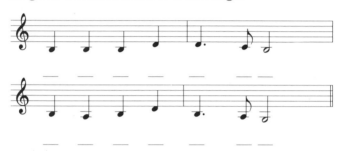

Scarborough Fair

The Bass Clef

Now take a look at the notes in the bass clef. This clef is also sometimes called the *F clef* because it forms a curlicue on the fourth line up from the bottom of the staff. Thus, the F note serves as a reference point for all other notes on the staff.

G   A   B   C   D   E   F   G   A

Take the time to memorize the position and name of each of these bass clef notes. Then write in the appropriate letter name in the space provided below each note of "Danny Boy." (The zig-zag symbol is a *rest*, or pause, which is covered in the next chapter.)

Danny Boy

Leger Lines

Now that you are familiar with the notes on the staff in the bass clef, take a look at the notes that extend above and below the staff. As in treble clef, leger lines are used here to extend notes beyond the staff.

Take the time to memorize the position and names of each of these new notes. Then label each of the notes in the popular tune fragments provided below.

Hark! the Herald Angels Sing

Westminster Chimes

The Ashgrove

Playing Notes on the Keyboard

Whether you are a singer, composer, or instrumentalist, it is helpful to know how to locate and play notes on a keyboard. Take a look at how the notes you have learned in treble clef and bass clef correspond to the white keys of the piano. The note labeled *Middle C* is the C note nearest to the center of the keyboard. Notice that many of the notes may be written in either clef.

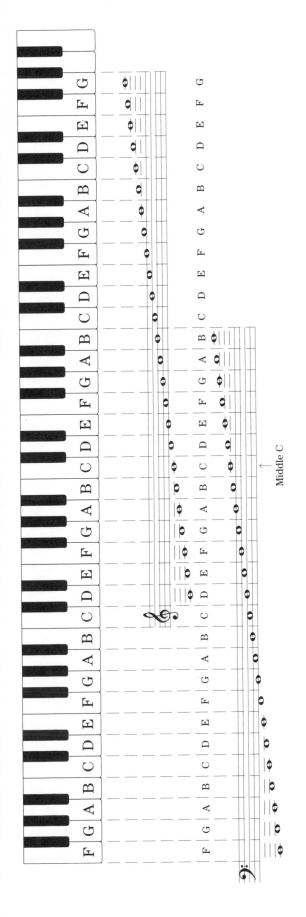

Playing Notes on Guitar and Other Instruments

If you play a treble instrument—like guitar, violin, flute, or clarinet—you'll probably want to place extra focus on reading music in treble clef. (Use a fingering chart for your instrument to memorize the playing positions of the notes you have learned.) Vocal music for soprano, alto, and tenor voices is also usually written in the treble clef (although a tenor sings notes an octave lower than written). Certain treble instruments—like clarinet, trumpet, and saxophone—sound lower or higher than the notes written on the staff. Guitar music is written one octave higher than it actually sounds. Here is a guitar fingering chart for a range of notes in the treble clef.

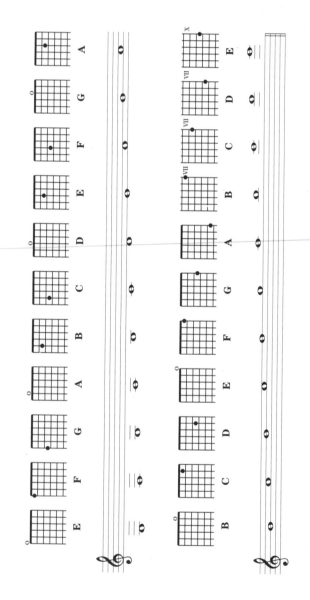

The Grand Staff

Pianists, in particular, should be quite familiar with the note names in both clefs. This is because music for piano is written on the *grand staff*, which is actually two staves joined together.

The staff with the treble clef is used to indicate music to be played by the right hand. The bass clef staff governs the left hand. The bracket that links the two staves together is called a *brace*.

The Octave Sign

Sometimes a composer or arranger intends for a passage to be played an octave higher than the notes shown on the staff. In treble clef, these passages are marked by an *octave sign* (a dotted line with *8va*, *8*, or *8ve*) above the staff.

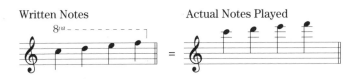

When an octave sign appears below the staff, the indicated passage should be played an octave lower than written. This inverted octave sign is only used to mark passages in bass clef (which are sometimes also marked with the Italian word *bassa*).

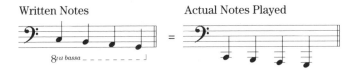

Octave signs are generally used to write very high passages in treble clef or very low passages in bass clef without using too many leger lines. This makes the music easier to read.

Note Values and Rhythm

As you have learned, the position of the note on the staff indicates a particular *pitch* (that is, how high or low a note sounds). Each note also has a *note value*, or *duration*, (that is, how long the note should last). The duration of a note is counted in beats. Here are the basic note shapes and their usual durations. Take the time to memorize the appearance and value of each of these notes.

   A **whole note** lasts four beats

   A **half note** lasts two beats

   A **quarter note** lasts one beat

   An **eighth note** lasts one-half beat

   A **sixteenth note** lasts one-fourth beat

   A **thirty-second note** lasts one-eighth beat.

An eighth note has three components. The circular portion of the note is called the *notehead*, the line is called the *stem*, and the tail at the top is called the *flag*.

The flag of the sixteenth note is made with two lines, while the thirty-second-note flag is made of three lines. Groups of consecutive eighth, sixteenth, and thirty-second notes are often linked with *beams*, as shown.

Eighth Notes   Sixteenth Notes   Thirty-second Notes

Stem direction is determined by a note's placement on the staff. In either clef, notes occurring below the middle line of the staff have stems that point upward. Notes that occur on or above the middle line should have downward stems. Although this is the preferable rule regarding stem direction, some printed music features notes on the middle line with upward stems. These occur only when other notes in the same measure feature upward stems. Notes connected by a beam should always feature the same stem direction (as determined by the natural stem direction of the majority of notes in the group).

Compare the different notes you have learned and their relative values.

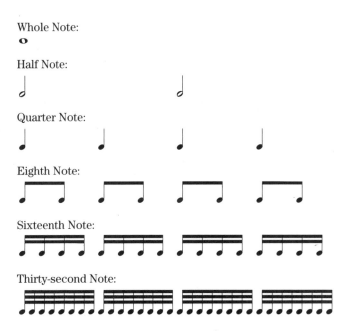

Whole Note:

Half Note:

Quarter Note:

Eighth Note:

Sixteenth Note:

Thirty-second Note:

As you can see, two half-notes equal the duration of one whole-note, four quarter-notes equal the duration of one whole-note, eight eighth-notes equal the duration of one whole-note, and so on.

In order to make it easy to count the rhythm of written music, the staff is divided into sections called *measures*, or *bars*. The vertical lines that divide the staff in this way are called *barlines*. A *double barline* is used to indicate the end of a piece of music. (A lighter double barline is used to divide important sections of a piece.)

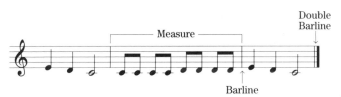

Take a look at some of the different note values in measures on the staff. Each measure in this example contains four beats. Count the beats of each measure aloud slowly and evenly while you clap the rhythm indicated by the notes.

The next example combines notes of different durations in each measure. Count the beats aloud as you clap the indicated rhythm. Again, be sure to count slowly and evenly without halting.

Reading a Song Melody: Pitch and Rhythm

Now that you are familiar with these basic note values, get ready to combine your knowledge of pitch and rhythm to read a familiar song melody. First count and clap the rhythm of "Jingle Bells." Then play the song on the piano, sing it, or use another instrument to play this melody slowly and evenly.

Jingle Bells

Rests

Music is usually composed of sounds and silences. The silent beats in music are represented by signs called *rests*. Rests are named and valued like the note values you learned in the previous section.

Whole Note	Whole Rest	
𝅝	= ▬	= 4 Beats
Half Note	**Half Rest**	
𝅗𝅥	= ▬	= 2 Beats
Quarter Note	**Quarter Rest**	
𝅘𝅥	= 𝄽	= 1 Beat
Eighth Note	**Eighth Rest**	
𝅘𝅥𝅮	= 𝄾	= ½ Beat
Sixteenth Note	**Sixteenth Rest**	
𝅘𝅥𝅯	= 𝄿	= ¼ Beat
Thirty-second Note	**Thirty-second Rest**	
𝅘𝅥𝅰	= 𝅀	= ⅛ Beat

Notes and Rests

Notes and rests may be combined in the same measure, as long as their combined values add up to the correct number of beats (in this example, four beats to a measure). Count the beats of this phrase as you clap the rhythm of the notes.

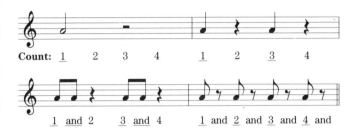

Count the beats of this next phrase as you clap the rhythm of the notes. Now play (or sing and play) this melody slowly and evenly.

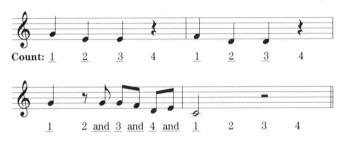

Pickup Notes

Certain song melodies require an incomplete first measure to provide for a *pickup*, which is simply a note or notes that occur before the first stressed beat of the song. When a musical composition features a partial measure containing a pickup, it usually makes up the remaining beats of the first measure in the last measure of the piece. This means that the last measure of the piece will also be incomplete. You can see how this works in "Polly-Wolly Doodle."

Polly-Wolly Doodle

Dotted Notes and Rests

A dot placed after any note or rest means that it should last one-and-a-half times its normal duration. For example, if you add a dot after a half note (which normally lasts two beats), you get a *dotted half note*, which has a duration of three beats.

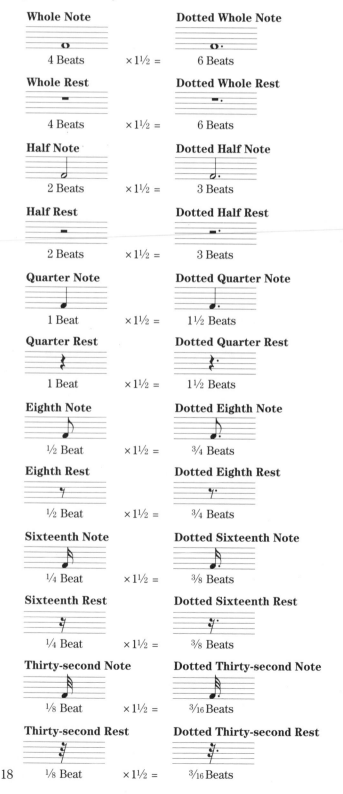

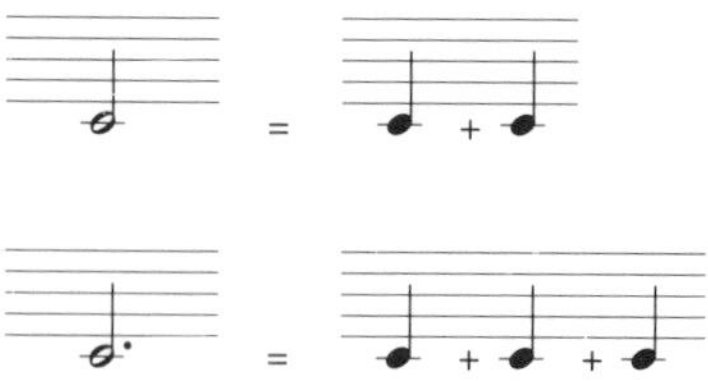

It's easy to understand dotted notes and rests when you compare them with the regular note and rest values you have already learned.

Whole Note		**Dotted Whole Note**
4 Beats	× 1½ =	6 Beats
Whole Rest		**Dotted Whole Rest**
4 Beats	× 1½ =	6 Beats
Half Note		**Dotted Half Note**
2 Beats	× 1½ =	3 Beats
Half Rest		**Dotted Half Rest**
2 Beats	× 1½ =	3 Beats
Quarter Note		**Dotted Quarter Note**
1 Beat	× 1½ =	1½ Beats
Quarter Rest		**Dotted Quarter Rest**
1 Beat	× 1½ =	1½ Beats
Eighth Note		**Dotted Eighth Note**
½ Beat	× 1½ =	¾ Beats
Eighth Rest		**Dotted Eighth Rest**
½ Beat	× 1½ =	¾ Beats
Sixteenth Note		**Dotted Sixteenth Note**
¼ Beat	× 1½ =	⅜ Beats
Sixteenth Rest		**Dotted Sixteenth Rest**
¼ Beat	× 1½ =	⅜ Beats
Thirty-second Note		**Dotted Thirty-second Note**
⅛ Beat	× 1½ =	3/16 Beats
Thirty-second Rest		**Dotted Thirty-second Rest**
⅛ Beat	× 1½ =	3/16 Beats

Take the time to memorize the appearance and value of each dotted note and rest. Then count the beats in the next example as you clap the rhythm indicated by the notes. (Notice how the dotted eighth notes are connected by beams to the sixteenth notes in the third measure.)

Now combine your knowledge of pitch and rhythm as you play (or play and sing) the opening phrase of "I've Been Working on the Railroad."

I've Been Working on the Railroad

You may also encounter a *double dotted note* in written music. Two dots indicate that the note is worth one and three-fourths of its normal value. In this way, a double dotted whole note lasts for seven beats. A double dotted half note lasts for three-and-a-half beats.

𝅗𝅥 = 𝅘𝅥 + 𝅘𝅥

𝅗𝅥· = 𝅗𝅥 + 𝅘𝅥

𝅗𝅥·· = 𝅗𝅥 + 𝅘𝅥 + 𝅘𝅥𝅮

Time Signatures

Every musical composition has a *time signature* at the beginning of the first staff. This symbol indicates two important facts about the overall rhythm of the piece.

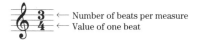

The top number of the time signature indicates how many beats there are in each measure. The bottom number determines which type of note is worth one beat.

> **2** = Half Note
> **4** = Quarter Note
> **8** = Eighth Note

The time signature is a guidepost to the overall rhythm of a piece of music. Each time signature also has a characteristic pattern of stressed and unstressed beats. In the sections that follow, you'll take a look at some basic time signatures and their characteristic patterns of stress.

4/4 Time

$\frac{4}{4}$ (pronounced "four-four") is the most common time signature used in written music. Much of the music we've examined in the book so far has been in $\frac{4}{4}$ time—with four beats in each measure and the quarter note lasting for its natural value of one beat. The $\frac{4}{4}$ time signature is so prevalent that it is sometimes referred to as "common time" and notated with a "c" symbol, as shown.

Each time signature has a natural, characteristic pattern of stressed and unstressed beats. The first beat of each measure in any time signature receives the most stress. In $\frac{4}{4}$ time, the third beat is also stressed, but to a lesser extent. "Jingle Bells" provides a strong example of the natural stresses that occur in $\frac{4}{4}$ time. (The stressed beats are indicated with boldface numbers.)

Jingle Bells

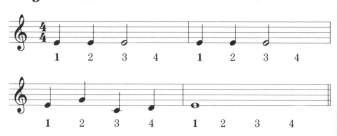

¾ *Time*

¾ (or "three-four") time is also sometimes called *waltz time*, since this is the characteristic time signature of this dance form. However, there are many other types of compositions that employ this time signature. In ¾ time, the quarter note still receives its normal value, but there are only three beats in every measure.

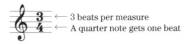

The natural stress of ¾ time falls on the first beat of each measure only. Sing or hum the first phrase of "Drink to Me Only with Thine Eyes" to get a feeling for the lilting stress of ¾ time.

Drink to Me Only with Thine Eyes

²⁄₄ *Time*

²⁄₄ time calls for only two beats in each measure with a stress on every other beat. Richard Wagner's familiar "Wedding March" illustrates the strong and regular stress pattern of this time signature. Notice the bass clef.

Wedding March

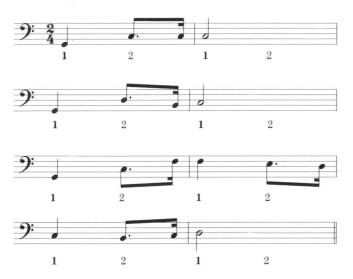

$\frac{2}{2}$ Time

$\frac{2}{2}$ time, or *cut time*, indicates that a half note lasts for
only one beat—with two beats in each measure. $\frac{2}{2}$ time is
usually noted with this shorthand symbol (¢). This time
signature makes it easier for musicians to read music
with many short note values or complex rhythms. Here's
the traditional fiddle tune "Turkey in the Straw" in $\frac{2}{2}$
time. Notice that the stresses fall on every other beat.

Turkey in the Straw

$\frac{3}{2}$ and $\frac{4}{2}$ Time

$\frac{3}{2}$ and $\frac{4}{2}$ time signatures also call for the half note to
equal one beat.

$\frac{2}{8}$, $\frac{3}{8}$, and $\frac{4}{8}$ Time

Some time signatures call for an eighth note to be valued
as one beat. Try counting aloud as you clap the rhythm of
these phrases. (Stressed beats are indicated with boldface numbers.)

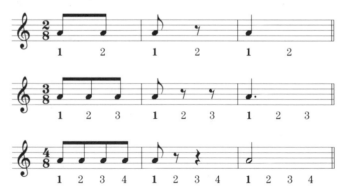

All of the time signatures we've looked at so far are
called *simple time signatures* because they require a
basic arrangement of the number of beats in each
measure and the value of each beat. *Compound time
signatures* will be discussed in a later section.

Accidentals

You are already familiar with those notes represented by the white keys of the piano: A, B, C, D, E, F, and G. The black keys of the piano keyboard provide pitches in between these notes. These pitches are collectively called *accidentals*. They are more commonly called *sharp notes* or *flat notes*, depending on their musical context. The names of these notes are formed by adding a *sharp sign* (♯) or *flat sign* (♭) after the note letter name.

Sharps

Let's take a look at the sharp notes as they relate to a portion of the piano keyboard.

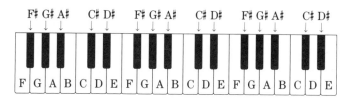

As you can see, each sharp key occurs just above the white key with the same letter name. Thus, the black note in between the C and D notes is labeled C♯. Notice that no sharp occurs between the E and F keys, or between the B and C keys. Here's the complete sequence of natural and sharp note names.

A-A♯-B-C-C♯-D-D♯-E-F-F♯-G-G♯-A

The distance between each of these notes is called a *half step*. A sequence of half steps is called a *chromatic scale*. Let's take a look at the chromatic scale, beginning on Middle C, as notated on the staff in treble clef.

Here's the same scale in bass clef, an octave lower.

Take the time to memorize the position and name of each of the sharp notes as they appear on the keyboard and staff. Then try playing these scales on the piano, or on the instrument of your choice.

Flats

Sometimes the black keys of the piano are viewed as flat notes rather than sharp notes. The reason for having two names for each of these notes will be clear when we discuss *key signatures* in the next section. For now, let's get to know the names of the flat notes. Flat notes occur one note lower than the white key of the same letter name on the piano keyboard. The flat sign appears after the letter name of the lowered white key to indicate the black-key name. Thus, the black-key note in between the C and D notes is labeled D♭. No flat occurs between the E and F keys, or between the B and C keys.

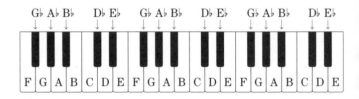

Here's the complete sequence of natural and flat note names.

A-B♭-B-C-D♭-D-E♭-E-F-G♭-G-A♭-A

Let's take a look at how the chromatic scale is notated using flats in treble clef.

Here's the same scale in bass clef, an octave lower.

Take the time to memorize the name and position of each of these flat notes as they appear on the keyboard and staff. Then try playing these scales on the piano, or on the instrument of your choice.

If a note appears with a sharp or flat sign, all subsequent notes in the same position on the staff of that measure are also affected by that sign. Note that the barline cancels both sharp and flat signs.

Naturals

A *natural sign* is placed before a note to cancel a sharp or flat sign used previously with that note. Once a natural sign has been used, all subsequent notes in the same position on the staff in that measure are natural.

A natural sign may be canceled by a flat or sharp sign. (Notice that the barline then cancels the sharp.)

Some pieces contain both sharps and flats. As a general rule, an accidental that leads up to a natural note is written as a sharp note—and an accidental that leads down to a natural note is written as a flat note. This rule is illustrated in "Melancholy Baby."

Melancholy Baby

Now test your ability to name musical notes by filling in the letter name for each note in the tunes below. Note the "unnecessary" natural in the last measure of the first example. *Courtesy accidentals* like this often appear as an aid to the reader.

Show Me the Way to Go Home

Shine On Harvest Moon

Major Key Signatures and Scales

So far, we've looked at sharp, flat, and natural notes that are individually added to written music. These notes are called *accidentals* or *altered notes*. Many pieces of music require that certain notes be sharped or flatted as a general rule. The number of sharps or flats that occur regularly in a piece of music determines the key. Rather than writing in a sharp or flat sign every time one should occur, these signs are written in a *key signature* at the beginning of each staff.

Composers and arrangers place music in different keys to accommodate the needs of the particular ranges of the voices or instruments for which they are writing. Certain keys are easier to play on certain instruments. Using different keys for the individual sections or songs in a larger work—such as a symphony or a Broadway show—adds variety to a performance. This is important to remember if you are planning your own concert, or writing music for others to perform.

The Key of C Major

Most of the musical examples in the book so far have been written in the *key of C major*, which has no sharps or flats. Thus, all the notes of the C major scale occur on the white keys of the piano keyboard. Once you understand the construction of the scale in the key of C major, you'll be able to build the scale and key signature for every other major key.

As you already know, the shortest distance between two notes, is called a half step. A *whole step* is the equivalent of two half-steps. Let's examine the pattern of whole steps and half steps in the C major scale.

C Major Scale

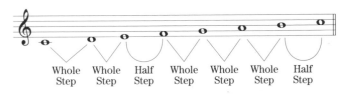

Whole Step — Whole Step — Half Step — Whole Step — Whole Step — Whole Step — Half Step

Take the time to memorize this important pattern, because it is the blueprint for all other major scales: whole step, whole step, half step, whole step, whole step, whole step, half step. Then sing or play the C major scale on the instrument of your choice.

The Sharp Keys

Once you are quite familiar with the step-by-step pattern of the C major scale, take a look at the *G major scale*. The notes of this scale are the building blocks for music in the *key of G major*. Notice that this scale requires an F♯ note in order to follow the proper step-by-step pattern for major scales.

G Major Scale

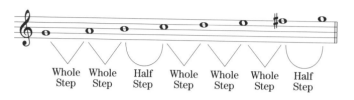

| Whole Step | Whole Step | Half Step | Whole Step | Whole Step | Whole Step | Half Step |

Since the F♯ note is a regular feature in the key of G major, it is represented in the key signature after the clef on every staff of the piece. This means that all notes that occur in the F position in the piece (unless otherwise marked) will be sharped—as in this excerpt from Schubert's "Unfinished Symphony."

Theme from the Unfinished Symphony

Keep in mind that the F♯ note indicated in the preceding key signature applies to all F♯ note positions in the piece, no matter how high or low. This applies to the bass clef as well.

F♯ F♯ F♯ F♯   F♯ F♯ F♯ F♯

Let's take a look at all of the major key signatures and corresponding scales that contain sharps. Although it is not necessary to include any sharp signs next to the notes of these scales, they are shown here in parentheses for your reference.

The Sharp Keys

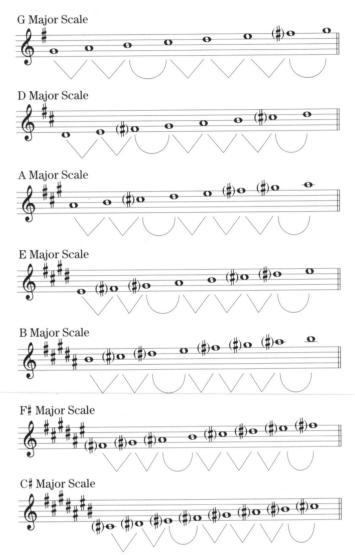

Here's a trick for identifying the major key represented by any key signature that contains sharps. Find the line or space position that is one half step higher than the position of the last sharp to the right in the key signature. This position names the major key. As you can see, this pattern is similar in both clefs.

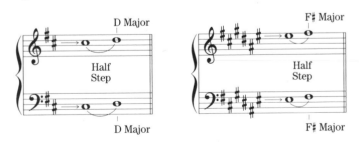

The easiest way to memorize the order of the sharps as they appear in the key signatures is to examine the pattern of sharps in the key of C♯ major, which features all seven sharps.

F   C   G   D   A   E   B

Take a look at the distance between each consecutive sharp in the key signature of C♯ major. Stepping down the staff by lines and spaces, the second sharp (C♯) is three note positions lower on the staff than the first sharp (F♯). The third sharp (G♯) is four positions higher on the staff than the second sharp (C♯)—and the fourth sharp is three steps lower than the third.

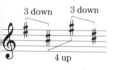

In order to avoid placing the fifth sharp of the pattern (A♯) on a leger line above the staff, this note is moved down an octave to the A♯ that occurs in the second space of the staff. The last two sharps (E♯ and B♯) return to the original pattern.

This pattern is identical in bass clef.

F   C   G   D   A   E   B

Familiarize yourself with the pattern of sharps. Practice writing the seven sharps that make up the key signature of C♯ major. Then write in the name of the major key indicated by each of these key signatures.

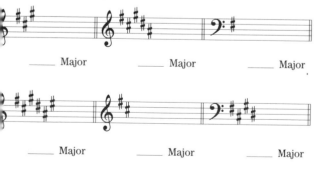

_____ Major   _____ Major   _____ Major

_____ Major   _____ Major   _____ Major

The Flat Keys

Now let's focus on the key signatures that contain flats. Here's the F major scale, which features one flat.

F Major Scale

Familiarize yourself with all of the major key signatures and corresponding scales that contain flats.

The Flat Keys

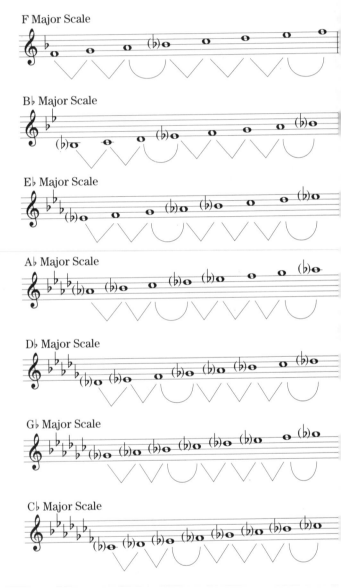

Here's a trick for identifying the major key represented by a key signature with flats. Find the second to the last flat of the key signature. Add a flat to the letter name of that note position and you've got the name of the key. (You'll need to memorize the fact that one flat indicates the key of F major.)

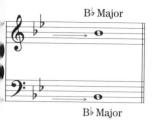

To understand the pattern of flats, take a look at the distance between each consecutive flat in the key signature of C♭ major. Stepping up the staff by lines and spaces, the second flat (E♭) is three note positions higher on the staff than the first flat (B♭). The third flat (A♭) is four positions lower on the staff than the second flat (E♭)—the fourth flat is three steps higher than the third, and so on.

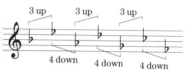

This pattern is the same in bass clef.

Familiarize yourself with the pattern of flats. Practice writing the seven flats that make up the key signature of C♭ major. Then test your ability to identify the major keys represented by key signatures that contain flats by writing in the key names below.

_____ Major _____ Major _____ Major

_____ Major _____ Major _____ Major

Compound Time Signatures

You are already familiar with the simple time signatures, like $\frac{3}{4}$ and $\frac{4}{4}$. *Compound time signatures* obey the same rules as simple time signatures, but the rhythmic stresses they create in music are based upon beats that are always counted in multiples of three. The top number of a compound time signature is always a multiple of three to reflect this pattern of stress.

Let's look at the most common compound time signature to appear in written music, $\frac{6}{8}$. As you can see, there are six beats to the measure, with an eighth note valued at one beat.

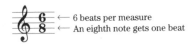
← 6 beats per measure
← An eighth note gets one beat

A stressed beat occurs every three eighth-note beats, providing two stresses in every measure. This pattern of stress is illustrated by boldface numbers in the first phrase of "The Irish Washerwoman."

The Irish Washerwoman

This same counting pattern occurs in music written in $\frac{6}{4}$ and $\frac{6}{16}$.

Time signatures that call for nine beats in a measure also create a stress every three beats. In $\frac{9}{8}$ time, there are three stresses in every measure.

$\frac{12}{8}$ time features twelve beats—and so four stresses—in every measure.

As with their "simple" counterparts, $\frac{3}{4}$ and $\frac{4}{4}$ time, the first stress in each measure of $\frac{9}{8}$ and $\frac{12}{8}$ time is generally the strongest. You may sometimes encounter complex time signatures—like $\frac{5}{4}$, $\frac{5}{8}$, $\frac{7}{4}$, or $\frac{7}{8}$—that call for unusual numbers of beats in each measure. These time signatures support different patterns of stress. $\frac{5}{4}$ and $\frac{7}{8}$ time are each illustrated below in typical patterns of stress.

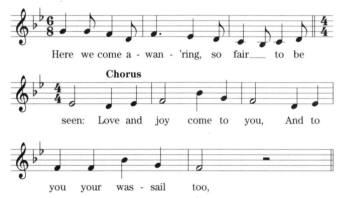

You may find that a time signature changes in the middle of a piece to create an entirely new rhythm. This can be seen in the traditional carol "Here We Come A-Wassailing." At the beginning of the song's chorus, the timing changes from $\frac{6}{8}$ to $\frac{4}{4}$.

Here We Come A-Wassailing

To familiarize yourself with the more commonly used compound time signatures, practice counting and playing these melody phrases.

Sweet Betsy from Pike

Barcarolle (from Tales of Hoffman)

Beautiful Dreamer

More about Note Values and Rhythm

By now, you are quite familiar with basic note and rest values. Let's look at some new note values and signs that express information about the rhythm of a piece of music.

Ties

Some notes are actually made up of two note values that are linked together with a *tie.* A tie indicates that a note be held for the combined length of the two tied notes. For this reason, the two notes that are tied together on the staff always have exactly the same pitch. Ties are often used to link two notes across the barline, as can be seen in the last two bars of this excerpt from "Daisy Bell."

Daisy Bell (A Bicycle Built for Two)

Sometimes tied notes are used within a bar to make the rhythm easy to count within a certain musical context.

Ties may also be used in sequence for this purpose.

If a note altered by an accidental is tied across the barline, the second note is also affected. Any subsequent notes of the same pitch will be unaffected.

Because of their similar appearance, ties are often confused with *slurs,* which are defined in the later section on accents and articulation. The way to tell them apart is to remember that ties link notes of the same pitch, while slurs always link notes of different pitches.

Extended Rests

Extended rests are used primarily in orchestral or band music since these genres often require that certain instruments rest for several bars. A numeral above the sign indicates the number of measures for which the instruments should rest. This sign indicates that the rest should last for twelve bars.

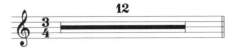

Pauses

Sometimes a composer or arranger wishes to indicate that the regular beat or tempo of a piece should hold or pause for a moment on a specific note or rest. This hold or pause is indicated with a *fermata,* as shown in the following two phrases of "For He's a Jolly Good Fellow." (The amount of time that the indicated note or rest should be held is left to the discretion of the performer.)

For He's a Jolly Good Fellow

Another kind of pause of indefinite length is indicated with two slashes above the staff (//). This marking is called a *cesura* (or *cæsura*)—and indicates that the note is held for its normal time value and then followed by an abrupt pause at the performer's discretion.

Triplets and Other Note Groupings

Composers and arrangers sometimes need to divide a basic note value into three notes of equal value. These three notes are collectively called a *triplet,* which is indicated by the numeral *3* on the beam. Each "eighth-note" in the triplet below is worth one-third of one beat. Try clapping the rhythm of "March of the Wooden Soldiers" (from *The Nutcracker*).

March of the Wooden Soldiers

Other note values may be used in a triplet. Here's an example of "quarter notes" linked in a triplet. Notice that a bracket is used when notes cannot be joined by a beam. Each of these is worth one-third of the value of a half note, or two-thirds of a beat. Play the first phrase of "Hey There, You with the Stars in Your Eyes."

Hey There, You with the Stars in Your Eyes

Triplets can also contain dotted notes and rests. Thus, in "Lilliburlero," the dotted "eighth notes" in each triplet are actually worth one-half of a beat. Each "sixteenth note" is worth one-sixth of a beat.

Lilliburlero

You may also encounter sixteenth-note or thirty-second-note triplets, as shown in this example.

Duplets do not commonly occur in popular music. They are used in music written in compound time signatures to indicate that two notes receive the value commonly afforded to three notes in that timing. The duplet in this phrase in $\frac{6}{8}$ indicates that the two "eighth-notes" are played in the time usually allotted to three eighth notes. This means that each note of the duplet is worth one and a half beats in this time signature.

Quadruplets, quintuplets, and sextuplets are also infrequent.

Tempo

The overall speed of a piece of music is called its *tempo*. Composers and arrangers often indicate approximately how fast a piece should be performed by using an Italian or English term on top of the staff at the beginning of a piece or section. Here are some common Italian tempo markings.

Lento (or **Largo**) = Very slow
Adagio = Slow
Andante = Walking pace
Moderato = Medium
Allegretto = Medium fast
Allegro = Fast
Presto = Very fast
Prestissimo = As fast as possible

Certain terms call for a changing tempo. The term *rallentando* indicates that the tempo should slow down. *Ritardando* (often abbreviated as *ritard.* or *rit.*) has the same meaning. *Accelerando* calls for a quickening of the tempo. The term *a tempo* tells the musician to return to the normal speed of the piece. *Rubato* indicates that the tempo should speed up and slow down according to taste.

The *metronome* is a device that taps out beats at regular intervals. The metronome's speed may be adjusted, and so it is useful to musicians for setting regular and precise tempos during practice. A *metronome marking* at the beginning of a piece or section indicates the number of beats per minute. This marking indicates sixty quarter notes per minute (so each quarter note lasts one second). This is a moderately slow tempo.

Compositions with time signatures that call for a half note, dotted quarter, or eighth note to equal one beat may include metronome markings with these notes. Each of the metronome markings that follow represent a moderate tempo (moderato).

Here are some other examples of metronome markings. From left to right they indicate these tempos: adagio, moderato, allegro, and presto.

Expression

Certain Italian and English words are used to indicate that a piece or section be played with a particular expressive quality.

Agitato = Agitated
Animato = Animated
Appassionato = With passion
Bravura = Boldly
Brillante = Brilliantly
Cantabile = As if sung
Con anima = With feeling
Con moto = With movement
Con spirito = With spirit
Dolce = Sweetly
Doloroso = Sorrowfully

Energico = Energetically
Espressivo = Expressively
Facile = Easily
Grave = Slow and solemn
Legato = Smoothly
Maestoso = Majestically
Mesto = Sadly
Scherzando = Playfully
Semplice = Simply
Sostenuto = Sustained
Vivace = Lively

Dynamics

Terms or symbols that indicate volume are called *dynamic markings*. Italian or English terms may be used at the beginning of a piece to indicate overall volume. Symbols are often used to abbreviate these words, especially when volume changes occur during the piece. Take the time to memorize these common dynamic symbols and their meanings.

ppp = Pianississimo = As soft as possible
pp = Pianissimo = Very soft
p = Piano = Soft
mp = Mezzo piano = Moderately soft
mf = Mezzo forte = Moderately loud
f = Forte = Loud
ff = Fortissimo = Very loud
fff = Fortississimo = As loud as possible

An increase in volume is indicated by the term *crescendo* (or *cresc.*). The terms *decrescendo* and *diminuendo* (or *dim.*) indicate a decrease in volume. Volume changes for specific notes are indicated with a crescendo or diminuendo symbol. A crescendo, followed by a decrescendo is indicated in the last four bars of "For He's a Jolly Good Fellow." (The relative length of these symbols indicates the notes included in the volume change.)

For He's a Jolly Good Fellow

38

Structure

In basic terms, a musical composition should have a clear beginning that leads to the body of the piece (often called the *development section*) and an effective ending. Many songs feature an *introduction* or *verse* section as an opener—leading to the *chorus* or main section of the piece. Classical compositions use various conventions for arranging the individual sections of a work.

Let's look at the different markings that guide the musician through the sections of a musical composition. The thumbnail examples used in this section illustrate the functions of these markings. In a full-sized musical composition, several pages of music may actually occur between symbols—so it's a good idea to review their placement and meaning before you begin to play or sing.

Repeat Sign

Most styles of music call for their individual sections to be repeated at times. In fact, this kind of repetition is often important to the structure of a musical composition. Two dots before a double bar form a *repeat sign*.

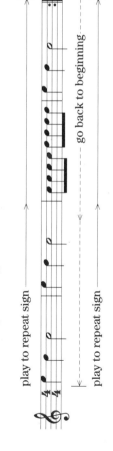

If a repeat sign occurs at the end of the piece, it indicates that you should repeat the entire piece once from the beginning. Play "Hot Cross Buns" twice through in tempo.

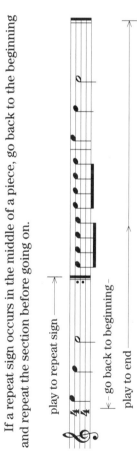

If a repeat sign occurs in the middle of a piece, go back to the beginning and repeat the section before going on.

Inverted Repeat Sign

If a reverse repeat sign occurs earlier in the piece, you should only repeat from that point onward. Here the inverted repeat sign means that you should skip the first measure when you repeat the piece.

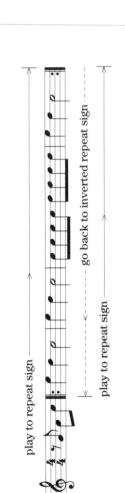

Da Capo

D.C. is an abbreviation of the Italian phrase *Da Capo*, meaning "from the head." This marking means the same thing as a single repeat sign—repeat the piece from its beginning.

Dal Segno

D.S. stands for the Italian phrase *Dal Segno* (pronounced "dahl senyo"), meaning "from the sign." *D.S.* means to go back to the dal segno sign (𝄋) and repeat the section.

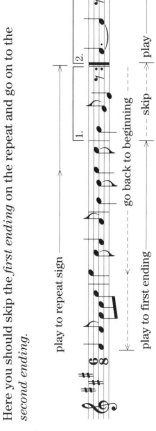

Alternate Endings

A bracket and numeral is used to mark alternate endings for a section. Here you should skip the *first ending* on the repeat and go on to the *second ending*.

41

D.C. al Coda

D.C. al Coda tells you to repeat the piece until you reach the coda sign (✜)—then skip to the next coda sign, and play the *coda*, a short ending section (literally "tail").

D.S. al Coda

D.S. al Coda means to repeat from the dal segno sign. Once you reach the coda sign, skip to the next coda sign, and play the coda section. *D.C. al Coda* and *D.S. al Coda* are also written *D.C. al* ✜ and *D.S. al* ✜.

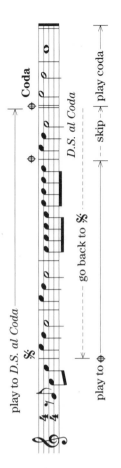

D.C. al Fine

Fine (pronounced "feenay") is the Italian word for "end." *D.C. al Fine* tells you to go back to the beginning of the piece and repeat until you come to the marking *Fine*.

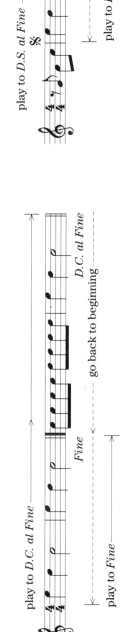

D.S. al Fine

D.S. al Fine means to go back to the dal segno sign and repeat until the point marked *Fine.*

Accents and Articulations

Different accents and articulations are used to create distinctive phrases and textures in a piece.

Staccato

If a dot appears above or below a note, that note should be played or sung with a short and crisp action called *staccato.* Staccato notes with upward stems feature the dot beneath the notehead. Notes with downward stems feature the dot above the notehead. In order to create a short, sharp sound, a staccato note receives less than half its indicated value. For example, each of these quarter notes is approximately equivalent to a sixteenth note, as shown.

Written Notes

Actual Notes Played

A triangle above or below a note also indicates that it should be treated as a staccato, though this marking generally calls for somewhat more stress.

Accents

Notes marked with any of these *accent signs* should be played or sung with a strong accent and held for their full note value.

The symbols *sf, sz,* and *sfz* (short for *sforzando*), as well as *rf* (short for *rinforzando*), indicate that a very strong accent be applied to the designated note.

Slur

A curved line connecting two or more notes calls for them to be played smoothly. The *slur* should not be confused with the *tie*, which calls for two notes of the same pitch to be played as one note value.

Sometimes a slur is used with staccato markings to indicate that the notes be played halfway between staccato and legato—that is, they are still detached, yet somewhat smooth.

Phrase Mark

A *phrase mark* is a curved line used by composers and arrangers to indicate the natural punctuation of a musical piece. Phrase marks are usually used to highlight longer passages than slurs, as shown in the first two phrases of "Twinkle, Twinkle, Little Star". Notice that a tie also appears in the last measures of this example.

Twinkle, Twinkle, Little Star

When used in a song, phrase marks often correspond with the natural punctuation of its lyrics. This type of agreement of phrasing between melody and lyrics helps make a song memorable and structurally sound.

Ornaments

Ornaments are musical decorations that provide points of interest in a piece.

Grace Notes

The *grace note* is a small note that adjoins a full-sized note. It is usually depicted as a small eighth note with a slash through its flag and stem. The grace note you will encounter most often in written music is the *unaccented grace note*. This note should be played as quickly as possible just before the natural beat of the note that follows. Here is the grace note, both as it is notated and as it is actually played.

A grace note that features an accent sign is called an *accented grace note* or *appoggiatura*. This note should be played as quickly as possible on the natural beat of the note that follows. Thus, the value of the grace note is deducted from that of the full-sized note, as shown.

Grace notes may also occur in groups. These are usually unaccented grace notes and their time value is deducted from that of the previous beat. A group of two or three grace notes usually features two beams, like sixteenth notes. Groups of four or more grace notes feature three beams, like thirty-second notes. Multiple grace notes should be played quite quickly, according to the skill and taste of the performer.

46

Trills

A *trill* is an ornament that consists of the rapid alternation of a note with the note above it. A trill lasts for the full length of the indicated note. Here is a quarter note with a trill, and an illustration of how the trill is actually played.

Longer trills usually include a wavy line after the trill symbol.

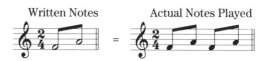

Tremolo

A *tremolo* is indicated by two half notes joined together with a beam. This means that these two pitches should each be played twice in an alternating pattern of eighth notes.

When half notes are joined with a double beam, the two notes are played four times each in an alternating pattern of sixteenth notes. A triple beam indicates that you play eight alternating thirty-second notes—which, in effect, means to play the alternating pattern as quickly as possible. Tremolos may be applied to other note values.

In music for stringed instruments, the term tremolo is used to indicate the rapid repetition of the same note. This figure is indicated with two or three slash marks through the notes stem, as shown.

Turns

A turn symbol (∾ or ∿) placed over a note indicates that a certain pattern of notes should be played or sung, as shown.

If a turn symbol appears after a note, the pattern begins on the second half of the beat.

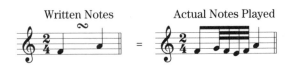

An inverted turn is marked with an inverted turn symbol (∾), indicating that the turn begin on the note below the written note. (The inverted turn may also be indicated with these symbols ∾ and ✝.)

If the inverted turn symbol is placed after a note, the pattern begins on the second half of the beat.

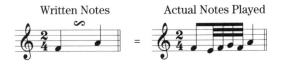

Mordents

The *mordent* symbol calls for the quick alternation of the written note with the note above it, as shown.

The *lower mordent* calls for the alternation of the written note with the note below it. This ornament appears more commonly than the mordent, which is sometimes called the *upper mordent*.

Intervals

The distance between two notes is called an *interval.* To understand how intervals are named, let's look at the *degrees* (or numerical names) of the notes of the C major scale.

1 2 3 4 5 6 7 8 (or 1)

Diatonic Intervals

Here are the intervals that correspond to the scale in C major. These are called *diatonic intervals.* Practice playing or singing these intervals until you are familiar with the name and characteristic sound of each one.

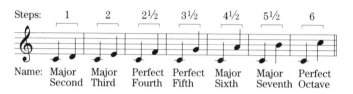

When the notes of these intervals are played simultaneously, they are called *harmonic intervals.* Listen to the notes of each interval played simultaneously on the piano or guitar.

| Major Second | Major Third | Perfect Fourth | Perfect Fifth | Major Sixth | Major Seventh | Perfect Octave |

Intervals may occur on different notes of the scale in different keys. It's easy to identify an interval by its position on the staff. For example:

 An interval of a second contains one note on a line and one note on an adjacent space.

 An interval of a third either contains two notes on adjacent lines or two notes on adjacent spaces.

 An fourth contains a note on a space and a note on a line with one line and one space in between.

 A fifth contains two notes on lines with one line skipped, or two notes on spaces with one space skipped.

 A sixth contains one note on a line and one note on a space with two lines and two spaces skipped.

 A seventh contains two notes on lines with two lines skipped, or two notes on spaces with two spaces skipped.

 An octave contains one note on a line and one note on a space, with three lines and three spaces skipped.

49

Chromatic Intervals

When a diatonic interval is made larger or smaller by an interval of a half step, a *chromatic interval* results. Let's take a look at the now familiar diatonic intervals and their corresponding lowered and raised chromatic intervals in sequence.

Chromatic Intervals (Lowered)	Diatonic Intervals	Chromatic Intervals (Raised)
Minor Second	Major Second	Augmented Second
Minor Third	Major Third	Augmented Third
Diminished Fourth	Perfect Fourth	Augmented Fourth
Diminished Fifth	Perfect Fifth	Augmented Fifth
Minor Sixth	Major Sixth	Augmented Sixth
Minor Seventh	Major Seventh	Augmented Seventh
Diminished Octave	Perfect Octave	Augmented Octave

One interval that has not been featured in the preceding charts is the *perfect unison*. The perfect unison may be diminished and augmented like any other perfect interval.

Diminished Unison   Perfect Unison   Augmented Unison

Take the time to memorize the name and appearance of each of the chromatic intervals. Play (or sing and play) each interval backward and forward until you are familiar with its sound. You'll find that certain intervals—like the augmented second and minor third—sound exactly alike. Determine which other intervals sound alike. (These intervals occur in a predictable pattern.)

When naming a chromatic interval, first determine the name of its unaltered form (second, third, fourth, and so on). Then determine the chromatic interval's name by ascertaining whether the diatonic interval has been made larger or smaller by one half-step (according to the major scale of the lower note).

Label each of these diatonic and chromatic intervals. Be sure to consider the clef and key signature of each.

It's easy to memorize intervals by associating them with familiar melodies. Here are some suggested melody phrases to use for this purpose. The indicated interval is shown in brackets. The common abbreviation for each interval is also included above the bracket.

The study and practice of intervals is central to a musician's ability to sightread written music. You may find it useful to study with a friend—and take turns playing, singing, and identifying intervals together.

Stardust   Oh Susanna!

Minor Second   Major Second
(Augmented Unison)

Greensleeves   Frankie and Johnny

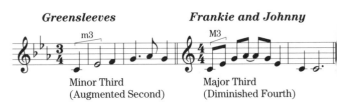

Minor Third   Major Third
(Augmented Second)   (Diminished Fourth)

Auld Lang Syne   Maria (from West Side Story)

Perfect Fourth   Diminished Fifth
(Augmented Third)   (Augmented Fourth)

Twinkle, Twinkle, Little Star   Let My People Go

Perfect Fifth   Minor Sixth
(Augmented Fifth)

My Bonnie   Somewhere (from West Side Story)

Major Sixth   Minor Seventh
(Augmented Sixth)

Bali Hai (from South Pacific)   Somewhere over the Rainbow

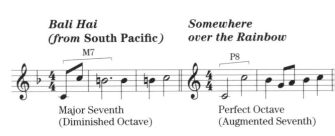

Major Seventh   Perfect Octave
(Diminished Octave)   (Augmented Seventh)

Double Sharps and Double Flats

Though they rarely occur, you may come across a *double sharp* or *double flat* in written music. These accidentals are seldom necessary—and keys that may require their use are generally avoided. However, double sharps or double flats are sometimes used to maintain a logical pattern of notes on the staff. A double sharp (✗) raises the indicated note by two half-steps. If the note is already sharped in the key signature, or by a previous accidental in the same measure, the double sharp raises the pitch by one half-step only. In other words, a double sharp raises any note two half-steps from its natural position. Thus, F✗ is another name for the G note.

An F✗ note is used in the following example to preserve the visual pattern of ascending thirds in the key of E major.

If a G note were used instead of F✗ in this passage, the pattern of thirds would be violated, and thus more difficult to read.

Sometimes a *natural sharp sign* is used to return a double sharp note to a sharped note in the same measure. However, a sharp sign alone is sufficient.

You may also sometimes see a double natural employed to cancel a double sharp completely in the same measure. However, a single natural sign is sufficient.

A double flat sign lowers the indicated note by two half steps. Here, B♭♭ is used to preserve the pattern of descending thirds in the key of E-flat major.

Minor Key Signatures and Scales

Sometimes a composer or arranger chooses to write in a particular key to lend a special tonal color, or *tonality*, to a piece. Many of the musical excerpts you have studied so far have been written in a major key, and therefore have major tonalities. A composer often chooses to use a *minor key* to lend an introspective or sad quality to a piece.

There are three forms of the minor scale: the *natural minor*, the *melodic minor*, and the *harmonic minor*. Let's compare the familiar C major scale with the minor forms. Since all C minor scales use the same starting note as the C major scale, they are called the *tonic minor* of this major key. For this same reason, C major and C minor are also sometimes called *parallel keys*. Notice that the third, sixth, and seventh notes of the natural minor scale are lowered by one half-step. The melodic minor features a lowered third on the way up the scale, and a lowered third, sixth, and seventh on the way down. The third and sixth of the harmonic minor scale are lowered by one half-step, whether ascending or descending.

C Major Scale

C Natural Minor Scale

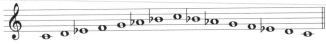

C Melodic Minor Scale

C Harmonic Minor Scale

In order to avoid the routine writing of the accidentals necessary to create these minor forms, music written in the key of C minor features a key signature with three flats (like the key of E-flat major). This brings the need for accidentals to a minimum. In this key signature, an accidental is required only on the sixth and seventh degrees of the ascending C melodic minor scale—and on the seventh degree of the C harmonic minor scale.

C Melodic Minor Scale

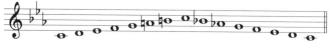

C Harmonic Minor Scale

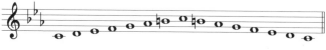

Because the key of C minor uses the same key signature as E-flat major, it is known as the *relative minor* of this major key. Correspondingly, the key of E-flat major is known as the *relative major* of C minor. Presented below are all the harmonic and melodic scale forms in every minor key. The name of each relative major key is shown in parentheses. Notice that the relative major key is always three half-steps (a minor third) up from the note named by the corresponding minor key.

Take the time to practice playing or singing each of these minor scales until they become quite familiar.

Sharp Keys

Key of A Minor (Relative Minor of C Major)

A Melodic Minor Scale

A Harmonic Minor Scale

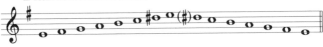

Key of E Minor (Relative Minor of G Major)

E Melodic Minor Scale

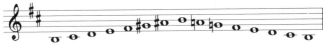

E Harmonic Minor Scale

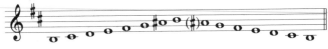

Key of B Minor (Relative Minor of D Major)

B Melodic Minor Scale

B Harmonic Minor Scale

Key of F# Minor (Relative Minor of A Major)

F# Melodic Minor Scale

F# Harmonic Minor Scale

Key of C♯ Minor (Relative Minor of E Major)

C♯ Melodic Minor Scale

C♯ Harmonic Minor Scale

Key of G♯ Minor (Relative Minor of B Major)

G♯ Melodic Minor Scale

G♯ Harmonic Minor Scale

Key of D♯ Minor (Relative Minor of F♯ Major)

D♯ Melodic Minor Scale

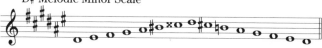

D♯ Harmonic Minor Scale

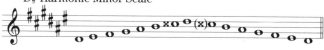

Key of A♯ Minor (Relative Minor of C♯ Major)

A♯ Melodic Minor Scale

A♯ Harmonic Minor Scale

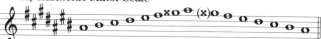

Flat Keys

Key of D Minor (Relative Minor of F Major)

D Melodic Minor Scale

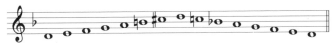

D Harmonic Minor Scale

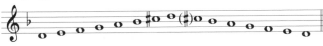

Key of G Minor (Relative Minor of B♭ Major)

G Melodic Minor Scale

G Harmonic Minor Scale

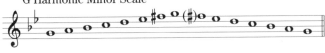

Key of C Minor (Relative Minor of E♭ Major)

C Melodic Minor Scale

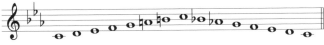

C Harmonic Minor Scale

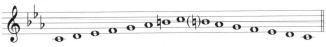

Key of F Minor (Relative Minor of A♭ Major)

F Melodic Minor Scale

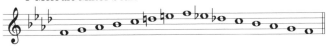

F Harmonic Minor Scale

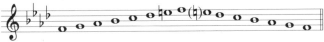

Key of B♭ Minor (Relative Minor of D♭ Major)

B♭ Melodic Minor Scale

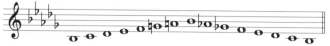

B♭ Harmonic Minor Scale

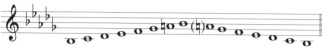

Key of E♭ Minor (Relative Minor of G♭ Major)

E♭ Melodic Minor Scale

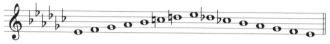

E♭ Harmonic Minor Scale

Key of A♭ Minor (Relative Minor of C♭ Major)

A♭ Melodic Minor Scale

A♭ Harmonic Minor Scale

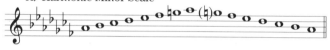

Further Study

Take the time to explore reading and playing the melody of your favorite songs, as well as ones that are unfamiliar to you. You'll find hours of enjoyment reading through sheet music and song collections as you strengthen these important reading skills. Be sure to refer to a complete chord fingering chart for your instrument as you read and play. You may also wish to pursue an in-depth study of chord forms and structure, as is provided in any good music theory textbook. This further study is also advisable for those who wish to compose or arrange music.

A basic understanding of the more advanced theoretical aspects of written music can only serve to enhance your music reading skills. However, at this point, you have all the facts you need to be a knowledgeable and competent reader. The music store and music library will provide you with many new doorways to a lifetime of reading enjoyment.

Answers to Written Exercises

Page
7   "Yankee Doodle"
CCDE | CEDG | CCDE | CB |
CCDE | FEDC | BGAB | CC ‖

7   "Aura Lee" (*Love Me Tender*)
GCBC | DAD | CBAB | C ‖

8   "Surprise Symphony"
CCEE | GGE | FFDD | BBG ‖

8   "Angels We Have Heard on High"
BBBD | DCB | BABD | BAG ‖

8   "Scarborough Fair"
DD | AAA | EFE | D ‖

9   "Danny Boy"
BCD | ED | EAGE | DCA | CEF | GA | GECE | D |
GCD | ED | EAGE | DCA | BCD | EF | EDCD | C ‖

10   "Hark! the Herald Angels Sing"
GCCB | CEED | GGGF | EDE ‖

10   "Westminster Chimes"
BG | AD | DA | BG ‖

10   "The Ashgrove"
G | CEGF | ECC | DFEDC | BGGG |
CEDCB | AFA | GCB | C ‖

25   "Show Me the Way to Go Home"
EEE♭EE♭E | CC | FFFFCDE♭ | E ‖

25   "Shine On Harvest Moon"
FE | FEC♯A | F♯FF♯E | D ‖

29   A Major ‖ B Major ‖ G Major ‖
F♯ Major ‖ D Major ‖ E Major ‖

31   G♭ Major ‖ F Major ‖ A♭ Major ‖
C♭ Major ‖ D♭ Major ‖ B♭ Major ‖

51   Minor Second ‖ Major Second ‖
Major Third ‖ Minor Third ‖
Perfect Fourth ‖ Perfect Fifth ‖
Augmented Fifth ‖ Major Sixth ‖
Minor Sixth ‖ Major Seventh ‖
Minor Seventh ‖ Perfect Octave ‖

Guitar Compact Reference Books

Here are other great titles in this series that you will want to add to your collection:

GUITAR

The Advanced Guitar Case Chord Book
by Askold Buk
68 pp AM 80227
ISBN 0.8256.1243.8
$4.95
Prepack AM 90176
$59.40

The Advanced Guitar Case Scale Book
by Darryl Winston
48 pp AM 91462
ISBN 0.8256.1370.1
$4.95
Prepack AM 91463
$59.40

Basic Blues Guitar
by Darryl Winston
56 pp AM 91281
ISBN 0.8256.1366.3
$4.95
Prepack AM 91246
$59.40

Beginning Guitar
by Artie Traum
64 pp AM 36997
ISBN 0.8256.2332.2
$4.95
Prepack AM 86997
$59.40

Beginning Rock Guitar
by Artie Traum
48 pp AM 37292
ISBN 0.8256.2444.4
$4.95
Prepack AM 37300
$59.40

The Compact Blues Guitar Chord Reference
compiled by Len Vogler
48 pp AM 91731
ISBN 0.8256.1385.X
$4.95
Prepack AM 91732
ISBN 0.8256.1386.8
$59.40

The Compact Rock Guitar Chord Reference
compiled by Len Vogler
48pp AM 91733
ISBN 0.8256.1387.6
$4.95
Prepack AM 91734
ISBN 0.8256.1388.4
$59.40

The Original Guitar Case Scale Book
by Peter Pickow
56 pp AM 76217
ISBN 0.8256.2588.2
$4.95
Prepack AM 86217
$59.40

Rock 'n' Roll Guitar Case Chord Book
by Russ Shipton
48 pp AM 28689
ISBN 0.86001.880.6
$4.95
Prepack AM 30891
$59.40

The Original Guitar Case Chord Book
by Peter Pickow
48 pp AM 35841
ISBN 0.8256.2998.5
$4.95
Prepack AM 36138
$59.40

Tuning Your Guitar
By Donald Brosnac
AM 35858
ISBN 0.8256.2180.1
$4.95
Prepack AM 85858
$59.40

BASS GUITAR

Beginning Bass Guitar
by Peter Pickow
80 pp AM 36989
ISBN 0.8256.2332.4
$4.95
Prepack AM 86989
$59.40

Beginning Bass Scales
by Peter Pickow
48 pp AM 87482
ISBN 0.8256.1342.6
$4.95
Prepack AM 90174
$59.40

Chord Bassics
by Jonas Hellborg
80 pp AM 60138
ISBN 0.8256.1058.3
$4.95
Prepack AM 80138
$59.40

Eight more Guitar Compact Reference Books available from Music Sales:

The Alternate Tunings Guide for Guitar	Guitarist's Riff Diary
Beginning Rock Guitar	Manual de Acordes Para Guitarra
Beginning Slide Guitar	The Twelve-String Guitar Guide
D. I. Y. Guitar Repair	Using Your Guitar

For further info contact your local music dealer or call: 914-469-2271
Music Sales Corporation • PO Box 572 • Chester, New York • 10918